Taken in by the Aliens

A Planet WLN269 Needs Women Story

Sabrina Cross

Cover Artwork by Anastacia N

Squibble Artwork by Kenzie James

Possum Artwork by Feraichi

Edited By: Writer's Wingman

Author's Note

While this is a fairly fluffy and short romance novella, there are still a number of topics that you might find distressing. Please take care of yourselves, loves.

This book contains the following: Religious trauma, poverty, mentions of child abuse and neglect, parentification of children, sexism and misogyny, attempted arranged marriage to a possible serial killer, cross-species dating, oral sex, vaginal sex, sex with multiple partners

If you feel I am missing anything please reach out to me at authorsabrinacross@gmail.com and let me know. A complete list can be found at www.sabrinacross.com

About Planet WLN269:

The United Civilizations of what humans call the Andromeda Galaxy had been fighting a war for centuries—one that had promise of ending soon...until it didn't. It took only one terrorist organization with a biological weapon to take out an entire civilization, leaving behind just one tiny mining colony on the edge of civilized space.

Fifty thousand men, one thousand women were all that was left–a mix that wasn't sustainable. How would these 50,000 men survive without hope for a future, a chance at offspring, or even just companionship?

It could have been the end, were it not for one stubborn woman who refused to allow her brothers to succumb to a life without the possibility of ever finding someone to share their life with.

She was sure her mission to find sentient life would be a lifetime sort of thing—instead, twenty-four hours after launching her search, she found Earth—and accidentally paved the way for the galaxy's most chaotic dating app.

With funding from Earth's governments and a questionable sense of what humans find romantic, the Human Extraterrestrial Liaisons Program (H.E.L.P.) was launched.

Much to the alien's surprise, Earth was full of women ready to leave their planet for anywhere but their current over-populated one. After all, Earth was home to a violent, backward sort of people who happened to have their own male loneliness epidemic—but it was one of their men's own making...

Chapter 1

Briar

G reetings Human Briar,
It is a pleasure to make your friendship. I am pleased you have accepted my suit and we may converse. I know little about your planet and people but I am eager to learn much from you.

Forgive me, I have never attempted to mate anyone before and do not know your customs. Please tell me about them. I would not like to offend.

You may be wondering why a male at my age has never mated, even before the fall of the United Civilizations. Rest assured, I am a sound mating partner. For many years, I focused on my education before moving to WLN269. And once here, there was much work to be done. Do not fear, human, I have *time and desire to make an effort for you. I shall be a good mate to you.*

With hope,
Sury

I read the compulsory courtship communication twice before handing it over to my friend Jules. Her brow wrinkles as she reads.

"It's English. Mostly." She tucks the letter into a box and shoves it under her bed. "I'm still not sure this is a good idea, Briar."

I play with the end of my braid and try not to squirm under her severe gaze. Jules has been against my application to Homosapien-Extraterrestrial Liaisons Program since the moment I brought it up almost a month ago. But she doesn't get it. Not really.

Jules and I were raised in the same church, which was the only reason I was allowed to be friends with her. But her family was far more casual in their faith. She had gone to public schools, and was attending college courses. She wasn't expected to care for her thirteen little brothers and sisters all the time. Her future husband wasn't picked out for her.

I fight back a shudder as I think about John Patrick. He was the biggest reason I had signed up for the off-planet dating agency in the first place. The moment our parents declared we would make a perfect match and began to encourage our courtship, I knew I had to get out of there.

There aren't a lot of options for a twenty-year-old without an education, diploma, job history, or life experience. Marriage is pretty much my only way out. Even if it means going off-planet to do it.

"What other options do I have, Jules? Marry John Patrick?" Jules shudders. In some circles, John Patrick is seen as a total catch. He's handsome enough, I suppose. But he's a total fundamentalist jerk. I'm pretty sure he's already imagining me pregnant and barefoot, waiting on him hand and foot.

"Okay, no, that's not an option. But, what if they're dangerous? We don't know anything about the aliens. And it's not like our government is trustworthy when they have their own agenda."

She isn't wrong. When the aliens first made contact months ago, the whole world kind of stopped. Everything we thought we knew went out the window, and we were faced with the fact that we weren't the most sophisticated beings in the universe. Not even close.

Panic had been wide-spread and the Earth froze as we all held our collective breath, waiting for the worst. But, as it turns out, the aliens need us. Their numbers were dwindling, and the men vastly out-numbered the women. No one official was calling it a breeding program, but everyone knew H.E.L.P was selling us off for our wombs. If that was all I was good for, I at least wanted to choose my husband.

"Can they be any more dangerous than human men?" It is a serious question. One I've asked myself over and over since I walked into the H.E.L.P offices and volunteered.

"I don't like it." It isn't an argument. There's none to be offered. "Okay, write your response and I'll send it when I go to class tomorrow."

Chapter 2

Briar

Hello Sury,

It's nice to meet you. I'm afraid I'm not the best resource for typical human customs. I don't have a typical human life. I suppose you could call me a shut-in. I promise not to be easily offended if you can promise me the same. I've never conversed with anyone outside my church before, and I'm afraid I won't be very good at it.

What kind of work do you do? I don't know anything about how alien planets work. Honestly, I don't know much about how any of this works. What made you decide it was time to take a mate? I assume mate means the same as wife to humans, but please correct me if I'm wrong.

· · ·

"Hello Briar, how are you this fine day?" John Patrick stands outside the church with his hands tucked into the pockets of his blue Sunday pants. I fight back a shudder at the casual possessiveness in his gaze. He's seven years my senior and should have been married already. The fact he isn't is a matter of gossip for the church ladies who come by weekly to help Mama. Most of them are certain he's just been waiting on the right girl. That they seem to think it's me is deeply worrisome.

"Hello John Patrick, lovely sermon today, wasn't it?" I try to keep my voice calm as I work to keep my siblings corralled. I do not have time for whatever this is. If we're not in the van by the time Father is ready to leave... Well, we'd just better be in the van.

Mama is home with the babies, which leaves me and my next younger sister, Isabelle, to ride herd on the rest of the children. Isabelle is barely eighteen, the largest gap between us siblings at almost three years. A pang of guilt hits me at the idea of leaving her the burden of the children, but then John Patrick picks up the tail of my braid and tugs.

"Indeed. The pastor was as insightful as ever." He twists the end of my long braid around his hand and raises it to his nose before finally releasing me. I fight back a shudder as revulsion hits me. "Say Briar, how about we grab dinner tonight?"

"I'm so sorry, I can't." I say, grabbing two of my brothers by the hands and hauling them toward the parking lot. "Have a great day!"

"Another time then," the smile never leaves John Patrick's face, but his eyes are flat above the curve of his lips. I pray Jules has another missive for me from H.E.L.P. soon. I can't allow him to become my future. And I don't know how much longer Father will allow me to keep putting him off.

Chapter 3

Briar

Dearest Briar,

    I have looked up wife and yes, there are some similarities to human wives. Though it appears our mates may be granted more autonomy than your wives. Are human women truly meant to be subservient? I do not think I would enjoy that in a mate.

    I am the manager of Village 57 on Planet WLN269. It is my duty to maintain order and productivity. A difficult but rewarding position to hold. Which brings us to your question of why I'm taking a mate. It is the responsibility of leaders to set the example for their people. I aim to help foster relations between our people.

    Tell me about yourself. How do you spend your days? What do you see for your future? Why did you sign up with the Ho-mosapein-Extraterrestrial Liaison Program? I wish to learn all about you.

Awaiting your reply,
Sury

Jules sighs as she reads over my shoulder. I know why she is sighing. She doesn't have to tell me that taking a mate for political motivations isn't very romantic. It's not. I know it's not. But I also know that I'm no better. I'm not looking for love on Planet WLN269, I'm just looking for an escape. He may be motivated by his position, but I'm doing the same.

"At least he's not looking for a house-keeper?" Jules says, taking the note from my hands to read it again. I pick up the pad of paper and pen and begin writing my response.

"Maybe he has one. Manager sounds like a high position on his planet. It could be he doesn't need a wife to take care of his house because he's got a dozen maids run-ning around."

Jules snorts and rolls over on the bed to stare at the ceiling. "I just want you happy, and I don't see how this is any different than marrying John Patrick. At least you'd still be nearby if things went wrong."

"He has dead eyes." I say, thinking about last Sunday at church, and the blank expression he gave me. "I'd rather risk my life with the aliens."

"Good, because that's exactly what you're doing."

Chapter 4

Briar

Dear Sury,

Wives are often seen as property. It's an unfortunate side effect of the patriarchy that reigns strong in our society. Please, tell me more about what is expected of your mate.

There isn't much to tell about me. I am the oldest of fourteen children. I spend my days helping Mama care for the littles. My free time, what it is, is filled with church service. I have never had the luxury of planning a future. I just want something different than what I have laid before me.

Do you ever wish for a different path? A different future? To break free of expectations? Sorry, I didn't mean to get so deep. Tell me about yourself. Did you always want to be a manager?

Sincerely,
Briar

"Get down here girl!" My father's voice booms up the stairs. He has nine daughters, but I have no doubt he's talking to me. He doesn't bother talking to the younger children. And he actually learned his son's names.

I set aside the laundry I was putting away and quickly obey, not wanting to anger him. Father didn't have the sins of many of the men in the church, but he had a wicked temper. And I knew the sting of his belt.

"What can I do for you?" I ask, trying to keep my voice neutral. I enter the dining room where Mama is making stew for dinner with the baby strapped to her chest in a sling. Some of my siblings are at the table working on schoolwork. And there, standing in the middle of the small space, is my father. He's beaming next to a smug-looking John Patrick.

"Your beau is here to see you." Father comes up and pats me on the back before giving me a shove in John Patrick's direction. "He's here to take you for dinner."

"Oh, but I'm in the middle of laundry and I have to give the kids baths tonight." I look to Mama but she's pointedly looking at the stove and not at me. "I don't have time."

"Make time." My father's voice is friendly, but there's an edge of steel under it. There's no getting out of dinner. I toy with the end of my braid and consider fainting, but I just know that would end with Father's slap on my face or worse. "Your sister can see to your chores."

He doesn't say which one. To him, it doesn't matter. Girls are only good for one thing—being useful to him. We're interchangeable.

"Let me get my shoes." I say, trying for a smile. It doesn't meet my eyes, but no one seems to care.

Chapter 5

Briar

Dearest Briar,
For my species, a mate is a partner in all things. We are equals. As it should be. I do not wish to insult your species, but they appear to have gotten this very wrong.

I was spoiled with choice. I am the only child and was encouraged to explore my options. I do not like your lack of choice. Perhaps we can discover together things that bring you pleasure. Maybe together we can find a better future. One we never expected to have.

With fondness,
Sury

. . .

"Okay, that's cute." Jules says, reading over my shoulder. "Are you going to go?"

It's a question I've been debating for days. The three month waiting period is almost over. My invitation to visit WL-N269 was sent over with today's missive. I knew it was coming, but I'm still unsure.

"That's the whole point, right?" It is. I know it is. But now that it's becoming a reality, I can't help but feel a pang of fear. Not only at leaving my planet and putting myself in the hands of a total stranger, an alien. But if I do this, if I go, I'll have nothing to come back to.

My father will not take this move well. I shudder as I think about the conversation to come. After dinner last week, it was made perfectly clear I'm expected to marry John Patrick and that it's only a matter of time before he proposes. I cannot be here for that to happen.

"Do you want me to come with you?" For a brief, crazy moment I think she means off-planet but no, she can't. She means to talk to my parents. And yes, I want nothing more. But they can't know about her involvement.

"No. Will you set it up? Tell me what I have to do next?"

"I'll make it happen."

Chapter 6

Briar

Whore. Harlot. Satan's Handmaiden.

My father's recriminations ring in my ears as I sit in the waiting room at H.E.L.P waiting for my final preparations for transport.

Women chatter around me, but I can't make out their words. It's just my father's voice in my head. I knew it wasn't going to be a pleasant parting, but I hadn't anticipated the level of vitriol. I open the last missive from Sury and try to find the hope it gave me the first time I read it.

Fear takes hold as the feminine robotic voice announces it is time to go. I watch as others gather coats, luggage, and personal items and wish I had more than the small, patched knapsack I'd filled with my few belongings. This is it. There is no going back.

I follow the group of nineteen other women out the door and down the long hallway to the transport.

"Please place your belongings on the cart for transport. Anything that is not worn or cannot be strapped to your person must go into the cart." My grip tightens on my knapsack, unwilling to let my belongings out of sight. Eventually, I set it in one of the carts attached to the ATV.

Once everything is stored, we are directed down a long tunnel to the ship. The first part of our journey is a three day flight to the moon. From there would be the flight to WLN269. In a matter of weeks, I'd be on a new planet with my possible future mate.

I hold onto that word. Mate.

I wouldn't be a wife, I'd be a mate. A partner. An equal. I wouldn't be a servant in my own home. I have to believe that. I won't make it otherwise.

Once strapped into my seat, I grip the third-hand jacket tighter around me and try not to think about the final scene with my father. The one that made it clear there is no going back from this.

"Welcome ladies, I know we've gone over safety protocols but we're going to do it one more time." The cheery blonde standing at the front of the transport reminds me of the astronaut doll I'd wanted as a child but never got. Her voice is endlessly cheerful as she goes over what to expect of the upcoming interstellar journey.

It turns out, talk of Gs, gravity sickness, and how to use the space bathroom. I'd read the paperwork front to back more than once after I'd made my decision to come. I know what to expect of the journey. I just don't know what to expect of what awaits me when we land.

Have I traded one bad situation for another? Is Sury everything he presents himself as or am I walking into something worse?

I look around at the other women and take in their bright eyes and wide smiles. Most of them look so excited to be there, without a care in the world.

Astronaut Brenda stops talking with a grin and a bright clap. With that, the door closes and the engines rumble to life.

Panic claws its way up my throat. I grip the harness and try to catch my breath. What am I doing? This is insane. There has to be another option. This can't be my only way out.

"I can't." The words are a hoarse whisper. The sound is silent under the roar of the engines. I bite my lip and swallow back the cry pushing at me. Tears well in my eyes, and even though it's too late in more ways than one, I want off.

"You okay, honey?" The woman next to me asks over the engines. I tilt my head to look at her. She's late thirties, with hot pink hair and a concerned smile on her round face.

I nod, trying to keep the panic at bay. A sob escapes and she holds out a hand to me.

"Oh honey, it'll be okay. You just remember your reasons for being here." I stretch out and grip her hand tight. Probably too tight. I can't bring myself to let go.

"What's your name, honey?"

"Br-Briar," The word is rough, but it comes out without the sobs. Progress.

"I'm Daphne," the woman says, squeezing my hand. "It's nice to meet you Briar."

I give her a smile, but I'm still not ready to talk. I'm afraid if I open my mouth, nothing but sobs will come out.

"It'll be okay, Briar. We're going on an

adventure. A big, terrifying adventure." The words strike me, and I look closely at her.

"You're scared too?" My whisper is barely audible over the engines.

Daphne laughs a little and squeezes my hand again. "We all are, honey."

Before I can think of anything to say, to ask any of the questions rattling in my head, the countdown begins.

Ten... Oh, god.

Nine...

Eight... No turning back now

Seven...

Six...This is happening.

Five...

Four... I'm going to be sick.

Three...

Two... Here we go.

One...

Everyone, including me, screams as the rocket launches and we're slammed sideways into our harnesses. Some of the screams dissolve into laughter. Some fall silent. And my sobs break free. Thankfully, I'm not the only one crying.

"It's okay, honey. Let it out." Daphne holds my hand and lets me cling while I cry.

"Thank you," I get control of myself and take a few deep breaths.

"You're barely older than a baby. What are you doing here, honey?"

I think of Sury's words and hold them tight.

"Looking for an unexpected future."

Chapter 7

Briar

Planet WLN269 is cold. Really fucking cold. The kind that carves down to the bone and makes a home there. As a Georgia girl, I've never experienced anything like it in my entire life, and I'm already dreading the years ahead; freezing to death in tiny chunks.

"Remember, honey. You contact me anytime you need to." Daphne gives me a great big hug before pulling away with a smile and a comforting grip on my arm. "Good luck, Briar."

With that, she grabs her large duffel and suitcase and goes off toward the entrance of the H.E.L.P. office where a snake-like alien awaits. The purple creature has four arms and four legs and large, bulging eyes. He's sinister looking and I can't help but worry for my friend.

But she seems happy enough, and he'd been quick to give me his contact information for their home in Village 32. I watch as he takes Daphne's bags in two of his hands before reaching out to wrap two around her waist and shoulders. Maybe he's not as bad as he looks.

I wait as other women are picked up by their aliens. And wait. And wait. It's dark by the time they finally call my name.

"Greetings Human Briar," I look up, expecting to see a large, furry, grey creature. Instead, I am face to eyes with a fuzzy orange basketball with lots of skinny limbs.

"Many apologies for my lateness." The ball says, exposing sharp teeth. "I am Mirk. I am here on behalf of Sury. He is unable to leave the unit at the moment. Please allow me to escort you to your new home."

They hold out a hand, one of four, but I don't take it. An uncommon anger rises in me. Sury had written of partnership, a hope for a future together. And he can't even be bothered to pick me up? I understand that as a manager, he has many responsibilities, but he had promised to make time for me.

"I believe I'll wait for Sury." I clench my coat tighter around me.

"Sury has been delayed and will be unable to collect you until tomorrow." Mirk looks around the space, filled with strange possum-themed motivational posters and old vinyl furniture, and grimaces.

"You may stay here. I shall wait with you. Or we could travel home and spend the night somewhere with more comfort."

I weigh his words. There is no scorn or anger in them. Mirk sounds simply resigned. I let the anger go and rise. What would be the point in forcing both of us to stay in this waiting room all night? I'm not that petty. I tower over the alien by more than a foot, and they're forced to lean backward to meet my gaze.

"Let's go then." I grab my knapsack and wait for them to lead the way.

"Please, let's get your items."

I push back the wave of embarrassment, and lift my bag higher onto my shoulder. "This is it."

A pause, and then the ball baubles a little and gestures toward the door.

"Let us go."

Chapter 8

Sury

My human is near.

I read the transmission from Mirk and fight back a shiver of excitement. And a wave of concern.

This is not the way I wanted to meet the human. But a cave-in at one of the mines put my people in danger, and I was needed. I shall make it up to her. Somehow.

Mirk told me of her displeasure, which I will weather. It is of no concern. My concern lay with the other part of his transmission. The human comes with but one small bag and nothing else. A frugalness I had not anticipated.

The humans were to be given a generous sum for relocating. Had the humans lied? I make a note to ask Lela about it later. I must now prepare for Briar's arrival.

My domicile is large, with five sleeping quarters. One is mine, one is Mirk's, and three remain empty. They are intended for spawn or visiting managers, but I chose the largest of the remaining quarters for my human. It has a large window that looks out over the planet's surface. The view in the pale night light is not much, but it is lovely during the day.

I pile the bed high with blankets and pillows. The color is pale and soft, as indicated by our human research. It is nice, I suppose, but I remain baffled at the human females' obsession with it.

Mirk hung cat posters on the wall, hoping to bring comfort and warmth to the room. I find myself relieved the human is not bringing live animals with her as their pointy faces and worm-like tails are quite unsettling.

My communicator chimes, and I don't have to look to know it is Mirk with an imminent arrival notice. I hurry from the room and to the door, where I wait for my human.

I do not have to wait long before the land transport enters view. I find I am very nervous. An emotion I did not expect.

Before the transport has parked, I open

the door and approach the vehicle. The top swings open and the passengers are revealed. There, beside my best and oldest friend, is the human Briar.

The first thing I notice is the ring of dark hair around her head. It is knotted and close to her skull. It reminds me of the fins of the Kav'lok people. And nothing like the images of humans I've seen in my studies. Next are her eyes, dark and large in her small, sharply-angled face. They seem to consume the space. And yet, she is lovely.

"Greetings, Briar," I say, moving to the transport to offer my hand. "My apologies for being unable to meet you, but I am very glad you are here. How was your transport?"

Chapter 9

Briar

The alien at my side is Sury. Though pictures did not do him justice. The male towers over me by more than a foot. His eyes are black pools in his wide, squared face. Sharp teeth flash as he speaks. He is wide and every inch of him is covered in pale grey fur.

I have an irrational desire to wrap myself around him and see if he is as warm as he looks. A shiver runs from crown to sole as chill seeps through my coat. I ignore the wave of panic the chill brings with it. My clothes, few as they are, will never be enough to survive in this climate.

Sury stares at me, hand outstretched and I realize he asked me a question. And probably assumes I intend to vacate the vehicle at some point.

Grabbing onto all my courage, I accept his hand and allow him to pull me out of the vehicle. His palm is warm against mine and I fight the urge to step closer.

"Hello Sury, it's a pleasure to finally meet you." And I almost entirely mean it. Even if there's still a kernel of doubt about this whole plan.

"Pleasure is mine, please come inside. Mirk will get your belongings."

"Oh but," I want to protest but Sury is already leading me away. I shove down the discomfort of someone else doing a task I am capable of and allow myself to be led inside.

Blessedly, it's warmer in the domicile, as I'd learned they were called. Though it is nowhere near as warm as I'd like. Sury probably runs hot.

"Allow me to show you my domicile." Sury maintains his grip on my hand as we tour his home. It's large and sterile with lots of metal and greys. It's also impossibly quiet. For a brief, crazy moment I miss the chaos of home.

"And this," Sury says, opening a sliding door by pressing his hand to a panel beside it, "Is your room. Mirk and I decorated it for your arrival."

The door slides open and I have to battle not to take a step back at the overwhelming pinkness of it.

The walls are a deep magenta with bright white lights tracing along the ceiling. A hot pink rug takes up much of the floor. The bed looks like a pink bedding factory exploded on it.

But the absolutely most bizarre part is the multiple possum posters on the walls. A mama possum with five babies on her back, a close up of a screaming possum, a possum in a pink tutu with a sparkly silver star wand.

"We hope you enjoy it." Mirk says, joining us in the hall.

It's a lot. Like, a lot. But this is my first time having my own bed, let alone a whole room. So yeah, pink vomited all over it but the bed looks soft and warm and it is all mine.

It isn't hard to say "I love it" and actually mean it.

Chapter 10

Mirk

"She is much smaller than I expected." Sury says, pacing a path around his bed.

"Taller than me," I point out.

He snorts. "I could wrap one hand almost entirely around her center." He waves a hand at me before resuming his pacing. "Did they not feed her? I'm beginning to think Isla has lied about the human females. She comes with few items and looks breakable."

I don't point out that his hand could span a lot of creatures. Or that the human ate much at dinner. Or that I too am concerned with her lack of belongings. And that she seems ill-equipped for our planet's temperatures.

Instead, I let him pace and rant while I

put together a task list for the next sun cycle. I add notes of Briar's preferences, as evidenced by our time together.

"Well, what shall we do?" Sury stands before me with his legs braced wide and his hands planted on his hips.

"I have made note to order clothing items and warmer outerwear from headquarters tomorrow. Also noted foods she seemed to prefer to make available at all times."

"What would I do without you?" Sury's face and voice are full of affection.

There are many things I wish to say, wish to do. But I swallow them all down and find the words he needs. "Thankfully, you shall never have to find out."

I push to my feet and drop the foot from Sury's bed, clutching my communicator. Before I might have offered myself to him. Might have brought him to pleasure. But no longer.

"Rest well," I say and leave his room for my own. The one I've only had for ninety sun cycles.

A part of me wishes to resent the girl, but I cannot. She was clearly ill-cared for on Earth. We can correct that. And Sury must lead by action. Many are still skeptical of the human program and Sury's actions show his approval. And his hope.

So no, I do not resent the girl. Not really. But I do have a moment of heartbreak when I climb into bed. Alone.

Chapter 11

Briar

I am never leaving this bed. It's like laying on a cloud. A warm, fuzzy cloud. But, from the soreness in my muscles and the fullness in my bladder, I've already been asleep a long time.

Finally, I wiggle my way free from under the pile of blankets. Cold immediately washes over me. I shiver in my cotton nightgown and rush to the tiny bathroom.

My toes are numb by the time I've finished washing my hands and face. I rush back to bed and dive under the covers.

A knock sounds on the door and I weigh my choices. Get back into the cold or invite whoever it is inside my bedroom. I wiggle my numb toes under the blankets and my choice is made.

"Come in," I call out. The door slides open and reveals Sury on the other side.

"Greetings Briar!" His voice is cheerful as he grins at me from the doorway. "We come with gifts."

It's only then I notice the stack of grey boxes with orange legs sticking out from underneath. It's a lot. My heart skips a beat. It's too much. Whatever it is, it's too much.

"Come in," I invite again, propping myself against the pillows.

Both males enter the room, Mirk teetering under the weight of the boxes. I curl my legs up as they set the stack at the end of the bed.

"We noted the humans failed to equip you properly. We have corrected that oversight." Sury looks excited as he hands me the first box. "Mirk assures me they should fit properly and assist in maintaining warmth."

I tug at the top of the box and find socks. Thick, fuzzy, socks in a spectrum of pinks. I run my hands over the impossibly soft fabric. Every part of me wants to tug them on right now. But there is no way I'm exposing myself in my threadbare nightgown.

"Thank you," I say quietly, stroking the socks.

"There is more," Mirk passes me another box and I am forced to set the socks aside.

That box was filled with a trio of pink sweaters. Warm, soft, and perfect. The next contains four sets of flannel pajamas. There are wool dresses, cotton tights, leggings, and a coat so warm I feel like I'll never be cold again.

Tears well and begin to fall as I look over the bounty of clothing spread across the bed.

"Oh no, we have done something wrong." Sury says. His brows crinkle together and he wrings his hands.

I try to tell him no, it's perfect. But a sob comes out instead.

"Headquarters assured me these were the proper items. I do not understand." Mirk looks at a communicator with a frown.

"No," I manage. "It's perfect. So perfect."

I hug the sweaters tight to my chest and battle back the well of emotions swarming through me. It was more than I'd ever owned. I'd never had anything so warm or wonderful before. They had noticed my need and corrected it without me having to humble myself enough to ask.

"But crying is a sign of distress." Mirk says, looking at his communicator again. "Surely, something is wrong."

"People cry for all kinds of reasons." I press my palms to my eyes to stop the flow of tears that are clearly distressing my hosts. "I'm just a little overwhelmed. This is great. So great."

Chapter 12

Sury

I exchange a look with Mirk, uncertain if the human is telling us a tale or if she is actually okay. Tears surely mean we did something incorrectly, right?

Briar removes her hands from her face and looks up at me. Her large eyes swim with liquid but they no longer fall down her face. She also has the sweetest curve to her mouth. Something deep inside me flutters at the sight of it.

It's not the warmth that Mirk brings me but something similar and all together new. Something only Briar brings. I enjoy the sensation even as I struggle not to evaluate it too deeply. I fear growing attached to the human who might yet decide the harsh climate of our planet is too much for her.

Mirk and I had both been concerned

when she slept for a full sun cycle but Headquarters assured us that many of the other women who had arrived with her were also sleeping extended times. When the motion sensors alerted us to movement, the relief in the room was a tangible thing.

I fear Mirk and I are both becoming too attached to the idea of the human. She is a complication in our relationship but neither of us can deny the appeal of everything she represents. We are no longer alone in the universe and our species won't all disappear. While I never much thought of spawning, even I must admit the idea of losing my species entirely is painful.

"Thank you," Briar says with a watery expression. Her cheeks are as pink as the walls and she still hugs an article of clothing to her. "This means a lot to me."

Mirk responds first, "It was our pleasure. Now, if you'll join us, we have much food in the dining room."

The color in Briar's cheeks flares even brighter pink. I examine her reaction with a tilt of my head and wonder what causes it.

"I, uh, I'm in my nightgown." Mirk blinks his eyes and clearly understands as well as I do. Which is not at all. The human sighs. "I'd be happy to join you but I need to get dressed first."

"Oh, of course." I make a note to increase the temperature in the domicile. Clearly she is cold and needs more clothing. "We shall wait outside, unless you feel comfortable locating the dining area?"

She gives me a sweet tilt of her lips that sends the flutters through my chest again. "Waiting would be great. If it's all right, I'll explore today but I'm pretty sure I'd get lost."

Mirk and I leave Briar to dress. Once the door closes behind us, I look down at my oldest friend to see my concern mirrored on his face.

"You did not tell me the human was treated poorly," Mirk says. "You must be careful with her."

I think back to the few messages we'd exchanged and realize I should have read more into her words. She hadn't just been busy, she'd been overworked and abused. I'd promised to help her discover her pleasure and I would uphold my word.

Maybe if we helped her discover happiness, she would stay.

Chapter 13

Briar

Life on WLN269 is terrifying. Not because there is anything particularly wrong with the planet. Thanks to Mirk and Sury I have plenty of warm clothing. The domicile also seems to be warmer in general. I no longer get numb toes going to the bathroom in the morning.

There is always something to eat in the kitchen without me having to ask and Mirk and Sury keep bringing me books and activities to try. I have everything I could possibly want or need, and I live in fear it will all be taken away from me.

"What shall we do today?" Mirk asks as I walk into the dining room for breakfast. There's already a plate of my favorites laid out for me. Mirk is finishing up some sort of lumpy oatmeal and I fight back a shudder.

After years of runny oatmeal, I never want to eat any again.

"Can we go see the Chiyaks again?" I take my seat and pick up my fork to dig into the fruit and something somewhat similar to yogurt. There was a herd of the tiny yak-like creatures just outside of the perimeter of the village.

"I do not understand the human fascination with Species 856." Mirk says, blinking all three eyes at me. "They are a nuisance."

"They're cute," I shrug and stab a dark purple fruit that tastes similar to cotton candy. "We don't have to."

"I have a few things to see to this morning, but we can go after mid-day." Mirk finishes his bowl and slides off the chair to put his dishes into the box on the wall that leads to the kitchen. Jules had been right, Sury has a number of domestic employees during the day that keep the domicile running.

Even after weeks on WLN269, I'm still uncertain how to interact with them. I've gotten myself in trouble for trying to do my own dishes and you'd have thought I'd suggested homicide when I'd asked about doing laundry. Sury and Mirk keep insisting I'm not to do any of the domestic tasks but I don't think I'll ever adjust to having things done for me.

"Sounds good," I try not to feel disappointed. Mirk and Sury both have important jobs keeping the unit running. I've seen them in action and know that they're needed elsewhere. But after a lifetime of household chaos, it's hard not to feel lonely with all of my free time.

While Daphne and I spend a lot of time chatting on the communicator Mirk gave me at the end of my first week, it's not the same as having my siblings around. And Daphne's Village is almost a full day's travel from Village 57, which makes in person visits difficult. Not that Daphne has any interest in leaving Ronds. She and her alien mate hit it off immediately.

I'm not jealous. But I am a little concerned. Sury, while always friendly and kind, has shown no interest in mating, in any sense of the word. A part of me is relieved. The rest of me is worried he will decide at the end of the three months that we're not suited and send me back to Earth. I have nothing to return to there.

"What is wrong, Briar?" Mirk tilts a little to the side, all of his eyes are locked on me, and I can see the concern there.

They've worked so hard to make sure I'm comfortable that I feel terrible feeling any discontent.

"A little homesick, I suppose." I say. It's not entirely untrue.

"Sick? Should I fetch the medic?" They grab their communicator, from the table, and I fling out a hand to stop them.

"No, not that kind of sick!"

Sury had insisted on calling the medics when I'd gotten my period, despite my insistence I was fine. The medic had been solicitous and ready to help but had almost no understanding of human anatomy. Thankfully, she had read the section on human reproductive systems and was able to assure the males in the house I was not going to bleed to death.

"I do not understand. What ails you?" Mirk keeps his hand on the communicator, ready to call for aid if I need it.

"I have thirteen siblings, I've never spent this much time alone before." I'm not sure how to explain the relief and loneliness warring inside of me. "I know you and Sury are doing important things, I don't want you to not work just to amuse me. But I'm kind of at loose ends."

Mirk hums but allows his hand holding

the communicator to drop to his side, rather than held at the ready to summon someone to fix me. "I will do some research into this problem. I have a meeting I must get to but is there anything you need first?"

"No, I'll be fine. I'm going to finish my breakfast and then go find somewhere to read." I give Mirk a smile and hope it's comforting. I really do like and appreciate the male. "I'll see you at lunch?"

"Indeed. Have a lovely morning, Briar." They give me a slightly terrifying smile, all those teeth, before leaving the room.

Chapter 14

Briar

Jules: So, have you been mated yet?

The message from Jules pops up on my screen, and I look around to make sure I'm alone. My face flames at the question.

Briar: Based on my research, Sury's species doesn't have a formal mating ceremony.

Jules: You know damn well that's not what I'm asking. Have you done the dirty with the space teddy bear?

I flinch at the blunt question. The movement makes Prince startle on my lap. I quickly move him to the ground before he poops on me. The chiyak is a nervous pooper. The day after my conversation with Mirk at breakfast, the animal appeared. He is Mirk's solution to my loneliness problem, and honestly, he is a great companion. We've bonded, and the puppy-sized yak follows me everywhere. I feel less crazy talking to him than I do talking to myself all the time.

Briar: No.

There's nothing else to say. The alien seems to have no interest in mating with me. He is kind and friendly, and I want for nothing. But he's never so much as looked at me with interest. I'd thought I was selling myself by coming here, but Sury couldn't seem less interested in mating.

I couldn't decide how I felt about it. My whole life I've been told it's my duty to submit to my husband and provide children. While I knew there was more to life than being a broodmare, I'd never expected to do anything else. My options on Earth had been so limited. And now I'm on another planet and have no clue what my purpose is.

Sury said he was mating to set an example for his people. Maybe just living with him is enough for him and his purposes. Maybe just putting on a show for his people to support the program was all he needed from his mate.

I know we are genetically compatible. H.E.L.P. did DNA testing as a part of the off-planet preparation, and I'd agreed to the extra mating screenings, knowing my worth was almost entirely in my uterus. Lord knows I don't have any other skills outside of raising children and homeschooling my siblings. But Sury has never mentioned any desire to repopulate his species. Maybe it isn't a priority for him. Or maybe he's waiting until the three month period is over and I'm trapped here.

I immediately reject the idea. Sury has been nothing but kind to me. Besides, even though we're only offered one chance at returning to Earth, the program has a lot of safety nets to prevent abandoning a human with an abusive alien.

Jules: I'd get on that. John Patrick is telling the church he'll still have you when you get this "little rebellion" out of your system and come home.

I shudder at the message. I have to make this work with Sury. Going home is not an option. My father will never take me back, and I cannot and will not marry John Patrick. Besides, while they gave us a small part of the stipend before going off-planet, the bulk of the money we were promised won't be mine until I become a permanent resident of WLN269. I need that money to help my siblings.

"Okay Prince, what should we do today?" I get up, tossing my braid over my shoulder. "Let's start with a walk and maybe see what we can find to do."

I lead the animal out of the room, grab my coat from the closet by the door, and leave the domicile.

An hour later, I'm wrist deep in dirt in the greenhouse. Prince is curled up in a beam of sunlight by the door as I work on potting seeds. The greenhouse workers have all gone home for the day, but I'd begged for a task, and Tierran set me up with starter seeds and pots. It isn't a hard task, and it allows most of my focus to be on the audiobook streaming to my headphones.

Daphne introduced me to romance novels during one of our regular conversations, and I'm addicted. All of the books I'd been allowed to read were church approved and heavy on morality and women's duty. Discovering an entire genre about women being loved, cherished, and cared for was nearly earth shattering. I couldn't read or listen to them when others were around.

Sex for the sake of pleasure was a foreign concept. Being on an alien planet was less outrageous than the idea any woman would actually like what happened in the bedroom. And it didn't just happen in the bedroom! In the books Daphne suggested, sex happened everywhere. In all kinds of ways.

I flush, thinking about the scene I'd listened to earlier in the day where they'd had sex on the kitchen table. Where people eat!

According to the church, sex was a woman's duty. It was an act to give her husband sons. According to my mother, it was something to be endured and was often over quickly. According to Jules, it was awkward and messy and not really worth the fuss. None of which matched what the books said.

Maybe they were romanticizing it. But Daphne seemed to enjoy herself with Ronds.

It's all so confusing. I wish I knew what was true and what was a lie. I didn't believe the church. So many of their lessons were small minded and filled with fear and hate. There was more to a woman than being an extension of her husband, and I had to believe there was more to sex. Mother's quick and fearful lesson on sex was based on her experience, but was that really how it was for all women? Father was a believer in the church's lessons on women, whereas the men in the books saw the women as individuals. It had to make a difference, right?

My head is spinning as I press seeds into the dirt I'd poured into the little pots. There is so much I wish I knew, and I don't know who to ask. Daphne would tell me, I'm sure, but how does one bring up a conversation about sex with a near stranger?

"What are you doing?" The voice is rough behind me. I jump and drop the pot I am holding. Spinning around, I see Sury in the doorway to the greenhouse. He's frowning at me with his hands on his hips.

I lift the pot upright and frown at the dirt on the worktable. I can't see the seed that I just pressed into it, and Tierran had been very clear that only one seed was to go in each pot. "Planting seeds."

My hands are covered in dirt, but that doesn't stop me from grabbing the end of my braid and twisting it. Sury looks angry, and I fight the urge to shrink back. He wouldn't hurt me. I'm almost confident of that.

"That's not your job." He moves forward, and I flinch. I can't help it. And guilt washes through me as Sury stops with a deepening frown.

"I know, I just wanted something to do." I wring my braids in my hands and try to hold my ground. "I didn't think it would be a problem."

Sury's still frowning as he looks me over. I glance down to see dirt on the front of my dress and fight the urge to try to brush it away. "We have people to do this. You don't have to do labor."

"I know," I shrug, tightening my hands on my braid. "I just, I wanted to do something useful."

Sury steps forward again, and this time I manage not to flinch. He's gentle as he lifts his hands to tug mine free of my braid.

He pulls them down, keeping them grasped in his much larger ones.

"You're getting your lovely hair dirty." He releases one hand and runs it down the length of my braid, brushing dirt free.

"I hate it." I admit. I want to take the words back as soon as they're out. Arguing with males has never been a good or safe idea. Sury just tilts his head and looks down at me with something like confusion on his face.

"Why?" He maintains his hold on the braid, stroking his thumb over the loosely woven strands. "It's very soft."

"It gets in the way. It takes forever to dry. It weighs so much that sometimes it gives me headaches."

His eyebrows draw together, and the frown returns. He stops stroking my hair and lifts it gently. "It causes pain? Why do you not remove it?"

I didn't know how to explain to him I've never been allowed to cut it. That my father and the church believed it went against God's will to alter any part of our appearance. That while other humans may have had the option, I was never given the choice.

Silence stretches on as I try to think of a way to explain something that makes no sense to most humans, let alone an alien. Sury drops my braid and cups my face in his hand, tilting it up until I can only see him.

"Would you like to remove it?"

"More than anything," I admit. Sury nods and steps back, finally releasing me from his hold. He looks around for a moment before grabbing a tool from the worktable. There's a slight humming sound, and he moves behind me.

"What are you..." Before I can finish my question, he's lifted my braid and sliced, cutting my hair off at the nape of my neck. I fall silent as he drops my braid to the floor, where it lands with a soft thud.

Oh. My. God.

"There, now it shall not bother you anymore."

My hair is gone. It is gone. The braid lay like a rope on the floor. Sury steps back around, setting the tool on the table as he moves. He's smiling at me as though he hadn't just chopped all of my hair off.

There would be no coming back from this.

"Now, how's that?"

I do the only thing I can do. I burst into tears.

Chapter 15

Sury

My stomach sinks as I watch Briar flee the greenhouse. Her little chiyak jumps up and gives me a look before chasing after her on stubby legs.

I had messed up. She said she wanted it gone, so I'd solved the problem. But it had been the wrong thing to do. Did I chase after her? Did I let her go? I had no clue what to do.

Mirk would know. Mirk understands the human in a way I do not. I exit the greenhouse and secure the door behind me before returning to the domicile.

I find Mirk in the dining room. The table is set for our meal, but the food has not been brought out yet. Mirk is typing away on his communicator when I walk in.

"I believe I have made a grave error," I

tell Mirk. I begin to pace the length of the table as I tell them about my interaction in the greenhouse with Briar.

"You did not think to ask her permission?" Mirk asks. They set down their communicator, all four hands fold on the table as they look at me like I am very dense. "How would you react if someone hacked off your fur?"

"She said she wanted it gone!" They're right. I should have asked first. My only thought was that it was finally a problem I could solve for her. My interactions with Briar, while pleasant, always leave me feeling like I should be doing more. Neither of us is truly comfortable with the other, and I do not know how to bridge the divide.

I can feel the time running out on us with every interaction. She still flinches away from me and has given no indication she would welcome my suit in earnest. If she cannot overcome her fear, I am afraid she will go back to Earth. That fear keeps me contained. I do not want to become too attached only for her to leave us.

"You truly are an idiot sometimes," Mirk says with a sigh. I pace the room, trying to figure out my feelings and how to solve the problem. I am good at solving problems. It is why I am so good at my job. I just don't know how to solve the problem of the human Briar.

Mirk says something, but I do not hear it as my thoughts swirl. Perhaps there is something I haven't thought of. Some way of proving to her she is safe with me. I have been as gentle as I can, but she still flinches.

What had the humans done to her to make her so frightened? Had they harmed her? My blood rushes at the thought of anyone raising their hand to my human. She is small and slight and should have been cared for, which she clearly wasn't.

And here I was doing the same things as the humans. Taking her choices away. Inserting my will on her.

"Sury," Mirk says, I spin around and find them standing on the table, bringing them to my height. I snarl at them, lost in my thoughts.

They snag two hands in the fur behind my ear and bring my mouth down to theirs. I freeze. The move is unexpected, but not entirely unwelcome. I have missed their touch. I have missed the press of their mouth to mine. I have missed their taste. I have missed them.

My hands go to his sides, between their

two sets of arms. I grip them tight and kiss Mirk back. We should not be doing this. Humans are monogamous creatures, and Briar would not like it. But I allow myself one moment to revel in his touch.

"Oh God," I jerk away from Mirk's kiss to see Briar standing in the doorway with a hand pressed to her mouth and wide eyes.

Chapter 16

Briar

The words burst out of me before I can think better of it. My hand flies to my mouth, but it's too late. They heard me. Two sets of eyes turn to me, all five of them wide in shock.

My heart hammers in my chest as I think about the scene I just walked in on. Hands and teeth and tongues. Oh God, the tongues. I've read about passion, experienced it secondhand through my books, but it was nothing like the intense kiss I just walked in on.

"Briar," Sury says, his voice trailing off before he looks helplessly to Mirk.

"Please, let us explain." So much makes sense now. The way they are so easy together. The fondness and affection they both share for each other. The fact that Sury has shown no interest in me.

Oh God, he never wanted me. I don't know why that thought brings me so much pain, but it does. A burst of fear hits me as I realize I'm going to have to go home. I can't possibly stay here when my being here is stopping them from being together.

"No, it's okay. It's good. It's great." I'm babbling. I take a step back, but Sury lunges forward to grab my arms.

"It's not what it seems." He shakes his head. "Or rather, it's very much what it seems but Mirk and I are no longer together. It was a slip."

"Why?" Why would they not be together when they clearly have so much chemistry? Why would they willingly choose to give that up? It doesn't make any sense to me. I'd kill for someone to kiss me like they were just kissing each other.

"For you," Mirk says, climbing down from the table to join us in the doorway. "Your presence is important and we want you happy."

I look between them. Sury's rapid nodding and Mirk's serious expression doing nothing to settle the butterflies in my stomach.

"But, you want to be together?" It's not really a question. I'm confident their answer is yes. I'm just not sure what to do about it.

I know the church says that same gender relations are a sin. I know I should be appalled at it. But if God didn't want males to love other males, why would He make them queer to begin with? It isn't like sexuality is a choice.

"It does not matter," Sury's voice is soft and sincere. "You matter."

"But you don't want me. Not really. Not like that." I gesture toward the table where they'd been kissing. My entire body flushes hot thinking about that kiss. That had been no dutiful peck. That was pure desire and passion. Things I hadn't known existed and couldn't help but want for myself.

"I want you here very much," Sury says, pulling me a step closer. I wrap my arms around my waist, but I can feel the warmth of him against them. "We both do."

I glance at Mirk, who bobbles in a semblance of a nod. Their eyes wide when they reach a hand out to me but drops it before connecting. Mirk's always doing that, nearly touching but not. A crazy, touch-starved part of me wants to reach out to grab their hand. To see what they would do.

"It's not the same." Wanting my presence to serve a purpose is not the same as wanting me. That was something I hadn't understood before. There was more to me than what I could be for others. I matter. My wants and needs matter.

"What would you have me do? Throw myself on a scared, damaged female?" Sury asks, his hands tightening on my arms.

"I'm not damaged." My back goes rigid at the accusation. I am a lot of things, but I am not damaged.

"The humans mistreated you." He raised a hand to my hair, now falling loose around my chin. "I have mistreated you. I am sorry."

My response is instantaneous. "No, you've been nothing but kind to me. It was just a shock. Another reminder that I can't go back home, to who I was before."

I reach up and grip his wrist, holding his hand against the side of my head. It's important to me that he knows he did nothing wrong. I hate that I've made him question or doubt himself. Other than Jules, Sury and Mirk are the only two people in my life who have ever thought I was more than an incubator.

"If you can't go back, let us be your

home." Sury presses a kiss to the top of my head. "Let us keep you. Oh no, you're crying again."

Sury releases me and backs up, holding his hands out in supplication. It's almost enough to make me laugh. Before I came to WLN269, I almost never cried. It didn't do any good, and my father was a big fan of "giving you something to cry about" parenting. But the emotional roller coaster of leaving home, Earth, and staring down an uncertain future has turned me into a crier.

"I can't stay here! Not if me being here is keeping y'all apart!" Something touches my side, and I look down to see Mirk's hand on my hip. This is the first time they've willingly touched me, and my heart stutters in my chest at the contact.

Chapter 17

Mirk

I touch Briar's side to bring her attention to me. With few exceptions, I am not fond of touching other beings. I am sensitive to natural energies, and contact is often painful. So, I brace for the jolt when I touch Briar, but none comes. Instead of the chaotic burst of energy of most beings, there is only a gentle hum.

It's not unlike the feeling I get when I touch Sury. Soft and warm, it flows down my arm and settles into my body. Pleasure fills me as I take it in.

Briar is looking at me, and I try to remember what I was going to say. The shock of her touch has addled my brain. I want to wrap myself around her and soak it in. I want to touch Sury and see how his energy compares to Briar's.

"Mirk?" There's a question in her voice, and I force my hand away from her so I can focus. Chill settles in, the moment I break connection. It's unlike anything I've felt before. Even Sury doesn't have this effect on me. I can't help but stare up at her and wonder if all humans have that effect or if it's just Briar.

"Mirk?" Sury sounds concerned, and when I drag my gaze away from Briar to look at him, his face is pulled down in a deep frown. Right. I was going to make a point.

I forgot what my point was.

"I'm fine." I say, as Sury's large hand comes to rest on top of my body. The gentle hum of familiar energy helps to settle me. "I'm okay."

"Are you certain?" Sury's frown deepens as he gazes down at me. His hand strokes against my curves, and I fight back a purr of pleasure. I've missed his contact.

"She hums," I tell him, knowing he will understand what I mean. We've talked about the way energy feels before and why I am able to touch him when I cannot touch so many of the others. He will understand how impossible and wonderful it is that Briar's touch causes no pain.

"Interesting." Sury says, his brow pulling lower.

Briar looks between us with a frown. "I don't understand."

"Mirk can feel energy. Kind of like a shock to the system, it's often uncomfortable." Sury looks at Briar with a wide grin. "Your energy hums. It is rare when they find someone that hums."

"They feel energy?" She looks at me, and I try to figure out how to explain something that we've been told humans cannot do. "Like static?"

"Somewhat," I say, not at all sure it's the same thing. But the frown on her face clears, and she looks more curious than upset.

"What does that mean? That you can touch me?" She hovers her hand over me without making contact. I reach up and grab her hand, pressing it to my side. I close my eyes as the warm hum of her energy washes over me.

"It makes you special," Sury says. Their energies combine inside of me in a sweet melody of feeling that almost brings me to the ground. I let out a small sound, and Briar pulls away.

I reach out and grab her wrist. She

freezes, but I don't release her. I can't get enough of the feeling inside of me. It's pleasure unlike any I've felt before.

My species doesn't mate. Not like many others do. We reproduce using a cell-replication process, and every being in my species is able to do so if the conditions are correct. While many of my kind can and do feel pleasure, mine is a very self-isolated species that does not often interact with others. I am an aberration in my choice to go off-planet, in my relationship with Sury, in the joy I find in pleasure.

While my species tend to stray away from physical sensations and focus on cerebral pursuits, I chase it.

"But, you two—"

"Why can't it be we three?" I ask, bringing her hand to my mouth to press a kiss against her skin. My lips brush against her flesh and tingle at the contact. "Why can't two things be true? We care deeply for each other. But we could care for you as well."

Chapter 18

Briar

"Wh-what do you mean?" I ask. My heart pounds in my chest as Mirk's mouth presses to the back of my hand. "We can't, that's not–."

Is that something that beings did? I don't understand. And yes, a part of me is terrified, but part of me, oh, part of me is so curious to see what exactly he means. Because, he can't possibly mean both of them. Together. That can't be a thing.

"Let us show you," Sury says, cupping my face in one large hand and tilting it up to him. I meet his eyes. The black orbs glitter bright, with something I don't recognize but still sends a jolt of heat through me. "Let us take care of you."

He lowers his head until he is just

above me, and I realize he's waiting for permission. I take a deep breath before reaching up to clench my free hand into his fur. "Show me."

Sury closes the distance between us, his mouth presses to mine in a gentle caress. His hand is warm on my face, his body hot under my touch. Mirk presses closer until their short, round body is pressed against my side and Sury's legs.

The kiss goes on, a gentle pressure against my lips. It's nice, pleasant, but lacks the sweeping passion that my books talk about. I'm about to pull away when he presses deeper, his tongue sweeps out to press against my lips. I gasp, and he takes advantage and slides inside.

It should be repulsive, but it's not. He's hot and firm as he strokes against my tongue. Jules had told me, my books had said, but I never imagined the jolt of heat that could come from such an act. My fist clenches tighter into his fur.

Mirk circles behind me and pushes my shirt up. His mouth presses to the base of my spine just above the waist of my skirt. He releases my hand, and I immediately grip Sury's fur to keep me upright. My legs shake at the sensations flooding my body.

"Tell us if something isn't okay." Sury says against my mouth. "We just want to make you feel good."

I nod, aware that the movement is jerky and slightly manic. Sury releases my face, and his hands drop to my hips. He helps hold my shirt up while Mirk keeps pressing small, hot kisses to my back.

Sury's mouth is back on mine, and his hands have risen so that his fingers press against the outer curve of my breasts. They swell and ache in a way I haven't experienced before. This was nothing like the quiet need that would sometimes hit me late at night as I shared a bed with two of my sisters. Nothing like the heat that suffused me when I read or listened to romance novels.

No, this burns through me and makes my skin feel too tight. I needed something I can't name or even fully understand. When Sury's finger brushes against my nipple, I gasp as fire shoots through me.

"Have you ever been touched before?" Mirk asks me, licking a path up my spine. I shake my head, unable to speak.

No, I've never been touched like this before. The secret place between my legs aches, my skin burns. A small, scared part of me wants to stop this and run away to hide. But oh, the brave part of me, the part of me that took myself off-planet to live with aliens, the part of me that devours romance novels by the dozens, wants this. Wants to finally discover what everyone else my age already seems to know.

"We'll take care of you," Sury says, lifting me up by my waist. I squeak and wrap my legs around his large center. He's so warm and soft between my thighs, but there is also pleasure there as I slide against him. "Mirk, table."

I don't understand until there is a large crash behind me and I crane my neck to see all of the dishes being shoved to the floor. Sury lowers me until my back meets the hard metal surface. I gasp at the cool touch.

"I don't know how this works." I admit quietly as Mirk climbs onto the table. He presses a kiss against my forehead with his wide mouth.

"Neither do we," Sury admits. "We'll figure it out together."

His large hands push my sweater up until it's over my breasts. My only bra broke since arriving on WLN269 and I haven't been brave enough to ask for a replacement, so my breasts are exposed to the cool domicile air.

"Fascinating," Mirk says, trailing his fingers over the curve of my breast and up to the tip, which has hardened to a firm point. "What purpose do these serve?"

"They're for nursing infants." I manage to get out through the fire racing through me at his touch. "Feeding our young."

"They're very responsive." He pinches the point, and I gasp, arching up off the table. He moves, and his tongue comes out to taste me. "Salty."

Sury, not to be forgotten, leans forward and closes his mouth over the other peak, taking it into his hot mouth. The contrast in temperatures and sensations is almost too much to bear. I tangle my hands into the fur of each alien, using them to anchor me.

"Oh, my god," I moan, arching against them. I press my legs around Sury, looking for friction but not getting any with the position I'm in. "Please."

I don't know exactly what I'm asking for, but they seem to understand. Mirk climbs back off the table as Sury presses a final kiss to my breast before circling around until he's at my head. I start to ask what he's doing, but he kisses me again.

"Don't worry, Briar. We'll make you feel better." Mirk says from my knees. He presses them apart. I fight against him, wanting the friction of pressing my thighs together and needing to keep what's between them secret.

"Shh, trust us." Mirk says, using all four hands to push my legs open. "I read all about human anatomy and breeding practices. They say you'll enjoy this."

I wasn't sure I trusted the literature they used to learn about humans. Not after the period debacle. But I am too distracted by Sury's mouth on mine and the feel of Mirk's hands on my knees and thighs as he spreads them apart to argue.

Mirk's fingers run down the center of me, and I jerk at the contact. No one has ever touched me there before. My first instinct is to slam my legs closed, but Mirk has a set of hands holding me open.

"You are damp here." He circles a finger around my entrance, where wetness has settled in my underwear. "That is good."

Sury lifts his head, and we both look down to where Mirk is wedged between my spread legs. They tug my panties to the side, and their tongue comes out to lick a path up my slit. I gasp at the hot touch of their tongue on such private flesh.

My hands clench into Sury's fur. He chuckles and leans down to whisper in my ear. "How does it feel? Mirk has a very clever tongue."

I have an idea of what he means, and the image it paints sends heat through me. I've seen penises, of course. I've been changing diapers since I was physically able to wrangle a baby. But I've never seen a fully grown male's penis. I shock myself at how much I want to.

Before I can respond, Mirk is back. Their tongue is long and skinny as it laps at my folds, burrowing deeper between my lips with every pass. Sury's hands come to my shoulders to pin me in place while Mirk's second set of hands hold my thighs wide.

"Show her, Mirk." Sury's voice is rough, but I don't look up at him as Mirk's tongue delves deeper and hits the bundle of nerves at the top. Living in a house with thirteen siblings, there's never been any privacy to explore my body, but I knew my clit could be pleasurable. I did not know it could feel like this.

"Oh, my god!" I gasp out as Mirk focuses their attention on it, flicking the tip of his narrow tongue against it repeatedly until I am fighting the hold they have on me. The sensation is so intense I want to escape it. My body shakes, and I feel completely out of control as pleasure so acute shudders through me.

Chapter 19

Sury

Briar's pleasure is unlike anything I've ever witnessed. Her entire body shakes as Mirk laps at her exposed sexual organs. She lets out sounds that shoot straight to my cock. I maintain my grip on her arms as she writhes on the table.

The flesh mounds on her chest shake, and I lean forward to take the tip into my mouth. It elicits a high-pitched sound from her that has my cock emerging from its sheath. I want so much to bury myself inside of her. She's so much smaller than me, and I cannot help but wonder how it will feel.

I suck her firm peak into my mouth right before her entire body goes taut. There's a moment of stillness before she arches up off the table and lets out a loud moan. My cock throbs at the sound.

"Delicious," Mirk says, pulling away from her. They look up at me with a wide grin showing off their row of pointy teeth. Their fur glistens with her essence.

"That was..." Briar's voice is hoarse and low as she seems to come back to herself. "I never guessed. I didn't know."

"It can get better." I offer, skimming my hand down the front of her body to touch her shiny sex. She's furred and the strands are soft and damp. She lets out a small mewling sound and arches into my touch.

"I don't know if I can take better." She says, flopping completely lax on the table. "That was more than I ever imagined. That was... mmmm."

Mirk gives me a knowing look before stepping out from between Briar's legs. She doesn't try to close them, just lays there limp and relaxed.

"Does that mean you are finished?" I ask, straightening and walking around the table until I can take Mirk's place between her legs. I curve my fingers under the garment blocking my access to her sex, and tug them down and off.

She helps kick one leg free but doesn't move otherwise, and I'm afraid we've gone too far. I tear my gaze away from the soft fur and shining folds to look at her face. It is completely slack and relaxed in a way I have not seen before. The lines of tension that almost always exist between her eyes are gone.

If I could keep her in this state of relaxation forever, I would. She is always lovely, but she is downright beautiful as she lies there open and relaxed for us. My cock is fully extended and weeping at the thought of being inside of her.

Mirk lacks sexual organs, and it has been a long time since I've been with anyone who has them. My palms sweat at the thought of sliding into the much smaller human. I must be careful, or I will hurt her. The last thing I want is to hurt her.

I run the pad of my finger through her folds and soak up her wetness. Her eyes fly open in time to see me bring my hand up to my mouth. She gasps as I suck her essence off of my digit.

"Use your words, Briar. I do not want to do anything you do not wish to do." I press down on the little bud of nerves Mirk focused on that seemed to bring her pleasure. She arches up off of the table with a moan.

"I don't have the words." She whines, pressing back up against my hand. "I've never felt anything like this."

I slide my hand down and press a knuckle into her opening, careful not to scrape her sex with my claws. "Would you like to feel me here?"

"Yes, God help me, yes." She arches her neck back to meet Mirk's eyes as they take my place on the other side of the table. "Please."

"So polite." I say, pulling my hand back and stepping forward until my cock can brush against her soft flesh. "Hold onto Mirk and tell me if it's too much."

Mirk climbs onto a chair and offers Briar their hands. She grips them tightly as I grip my cock and slide it down toward her entrance. The deep purple contrasts against the pale pink of her sex, and I take a moment to appreciate the visual.

"Sury, please. It aches." Briar arches against me. The movement notches my tip at her entrance and makes me groan deep in my chest.

"We'll make it feel all better." I promise

before pressing the pointed head of my cock into her warm opening. I press forward, but there is some kind of barrier that stretches around me. She gasps and goes rigid. "Should I stop?"

"No," The denial is instant. "Don't stop. It'll be okay. Don't stop."

Still, she is tense. I grip her thighs, uncertain how to proceed. Mirk seems to understand something I do not because they climb from the chair to the table and, while keeping grip on Briar's hands, straddle her torso. Their long tongue comes out and they flick it against the pleasure bump. Briar gasps, and I can feel her relax under my touch.

This time when I move forward, there is no resistance. I press inside slowly, giving Briar time to adjust. My gaze is locked on where we are joined. It feels indescribable. So tight and wet and so different from Mirk's mouth.

"There's a good human, taking my cock so deep." I mutter as the last of my cock disappears inside of her pink channel. Mirk's tongue abandons her bump and flicks the base of my cock before he returns to Briar and her pleasure.

"It's so much." Briar whines, squirming against me. "But feels so good. Please don't stop."

"No, little human. This is just the beginning."

Chapter 20

Briar

The stretch inside of me is almost too much as Sury pulls out of me slowly and eases back in. I clench Mirk's hands in mine and try not to worry about hurting them as I try to ground myself against the onslaught of sensation. Pressure, pleasure, stretch nearly to the point of discomfort all battle it out inside of me as Sury moves.

The flick of Mirk's tongue is nearly overwhelming in and of itself. My clit is so sensitive from their earlier attention. I want to tell them to stop, but I can't get enough air in my lungs. My entire body flashes hot and tenses in a way that's familiar but still so strange.

I'm going to come. My nails dig into Mirk's hands as I try to move. I need to move. But there's no room between Mirk on my chest, Sury gripping my hips, and the death grip I have on Mirk's hands. There's nowhere for me to go as pleasure overwhelms me.

Sury's movements speed up as he moves inside of me, and a part of me wishes I could see what that looks like. Is his penis different from a human's? It would have to be, right? I nearly giggle at the insane, inane thought, but my mind is fractured.

Mirk adds pressure to my clit, and I moan. My entire body clenches. Sury's invasion feels almost impossible as my inner muscles tighten around him. His hands grip harder, and he moves faster. Faster. Faster.

His penis hits something inside of me, and it's all over. My body explodes with pleasure as I come again on a moan. He doesn't stop moving. Instead, he pounds into me harder and faster, chasing his own pleasure. It's too much. I want to shove them away. To beg them to stop. To do something other than lay trapped there to take it.

Mirk shifts, and their fur rubs against my tight nipples. The pleasure is so acute it borders on pain. I try to shift away, but there's nowhere to go. Nothing to do but endure.

It isn't long before my body tightens again. Impossibly. Painfully. Amazingly. Oh. Oh fuck. Oh Christ. Oh God.

Oh. Oh. Oh. Oh God.

I come again. This time, Sury comes with me. He thrusts deep and freezes, his penis pulsing inside of me. It's unlike anything I've felt before.

This time, when I go slack, Mirk and Sury don't keep pushing. Every muscle in my body feels like water, and I'm barely able to open my eyes. Mirk releases my hands and climbs off of me. There's rumbling as Mirk and Sury talk, but I'm too drained to process the words.

I don't know how long I float there before something warm and soft is draped over me. Before I'm pulled off the table and up against Sury's hot, fuzzy body.

"Are you still with us?" He asks as he carries me somewhere. I mumble something unintelligible into his fur, and he laughs. The sound vibrates through me, a comfortable feeling I want to sink into.

"You took me so well." Sury says. I peek open at the whoosh of the door and realize he brought me to his room. His bed is more than twice the size of the one in my room and is covered in a dark brown blanket. I glance down and find myself covered in one of the many pink blankets from my bed.

Neither of us says anything as Sury climbs into bed with me in his arms. He helps settle me on his lap with the blanket wrapped around me. My entire body is beginning to ache a little, and the place between my legs is sore. But it's not an unpleasant sort of sore.

"How is she?" Mirk asks, coming into the room with a tray. They set it on the bedside table and pour out a glass of water that I gratefully accept.

"Never better," I tell them before taking a deep swallow of water. I nearly moan as the cool liquid soothes my sore throat.

"Very good," they say before taking the glass away from me and climbing onto the bed as well. "We were a little worried when you went limp."

"It was a lot," I admit. I shift so they can snuggle up against Sury's side. They take my legs and drape them across his lap. "I've never. I didn't imagine. I..."

I give up. I don't have the words to explain everything that just happened and the way I feel in this moment. They seem to understand because neither pushes me to go on. We just settle onto the bed in a comfortable silence that seeps into my very soul.

Sury rubs an idle hand up and down my back as I lie in the crook of his arm. Mirk rubs a similar path up and down my shins and calves. I float in the warmth and touch until I finally fade off to sleep.

Briar

Mirk's hands wrap around my hips, and I swat them away with a laugh. I finish putting away my clothing in the drawer and turn to glare down at him with my hands on my hips.

"No funny business," I say firmly. The effect is somewhat minimized by the twitch of my lips as Mirk glares at me. "I want this done before Sury gets back."

Sury was called away to Headquarters two days ago and messaged to say he'd be back for dinner. Mirk has been in charge while he's been gone, and I'm looking forward to having some time alone with both of my aliens.

"The work will remain tomorrow." Mirk says, sliding a set of hands up under the hem of my skirt. "Meanwhile, I have not tasted you since yesterday."

"You're a pussy addict." I say, laughing as I swat their hands away again. "I'm working in the greenhouse tomorrow. So I want this done today."

"There is domicile staff that can see to it."

"I can see to it." I argue. I did allow the staff to wash my clothing because I could not figure out the insane washing machine, but I still am not comfortable with people doing everything for me. I don't think I ever will be.

"You're killing me." Mirk whines. I bend down to press a kiss to their top, before grabbing another stack of neatly folded clothes. "Why are your clothes still in this room? You no longer sleep here."

"Because it's easier to dress here than rearrange our room to fit the dresser." Which is partially true. "Plus I like my shower better."

Sury's is large enough to fit all three of us with room to maneuver. Which is fantastic in many circumstances, but it feels too large and empty when it's just me. Easier to just keep my space for now.

"Harrumph." Mirk says, folding both

sets of arms over their chest. I try not to smile as I put the last of my things away. "Fine. But you're mine the second Sury returns."

"The very moment," I promise them with another brief kiss and a pat. "Now leave me alone and go find something to do."

"Bossy." They blow me a kiss and disappear out the door. I find myself standing in the middle of my room grinning.

"How is this my life?" I ask myself as I grab my communicator and open my messages.

Just a few months ago I never could have dreamed of the life I have now. Of the happiness and joy and sheer amount of love I am surrounded in. While I still miss my family and Jules, I can't regret a single thing that brought me here.

There's a message from H.E.L.P. in the top of my messages. I read over the missive, and my heart stutters. This is it. It's been three months on WLN269 and it's time to plan my return to Earth if I'm dissatisfied. Which means Sury will have gotten the same message about sending me away.

For a brief moment, panic hits, and I think about him sending me away, but I stamp it out. He wouldn't do that. Even if we hadn't found our way into bed together, Sury would never send me back. He understood how bad things were for me on Earth, and he would never send me back to that.

I save the message for later and skip to the next one. It's from Jules.

Don't Panic! It started. Which, of course, instantly makes me panic.

Isabelle is safe with me, but your father tried to sell her off to John Patrick. I got her out the moment the news hit, and she's staying with me until we can get her settled somewhere. We're working on getting a GED and maybe getting her into college classes. About time one of you went to university.

JP confronted your father about the loss of a second bride, and I guess it was really ugly. Your father has a couple broken bones. JP has more. JP's mom bailed him out, but, of course, your mother couldn't afford to bail your dad out, so he's stuck for now.

I miss you. Tell me everything that's happening up there. Maybe once I've got Isabelle settled, I'll sign up. Seems dating spacemen is the way to go. Lord knows there's no hope for these human men!

Love you!

Jules

I read the message. And again. I'm in total shock. Earth has gone crazy.

I'm still contemplating my response when Mirk sticks their head in the door. "Sury just arrived. You're ours."

The toothy smile they give me might have scared me once upon a time, but now I just set my communicator aside and push to my feet. Excitement surges through me as I cross and grab Mirk's hand.

I'd run away from a terrible life on Earth, certain I was selling myself into the same fate. Instead, I'd found myself not one, but two aliens who cared for me and my happiness. It was more than I could have ever hoped for. Joy fills my chest as we head out of my bedroom to find our third.

"Let's go get him."

Planet WLN269 Needs Women Series Titles:

Planet WLN269 Needs Women: A Prequel by Dakota Cockaday writing as Cassi O. Peia

Home, Home on the Strange by May Furhst

Going Batty for You by E.K. Darnell

Filling the Void While Also Being Filled by the Void by Ginger Kane

Alotl Love to Share by Holly Hanzo

Taken in by the Aliens by Sabrina Cross

Love & Other Squibbles by Kenzie James

Planet WLN269 Needs Women Series Titles:

Between a Rock and a Hard Place by Elsie LePlant

Tangled in his Tides by April Showers

Danth, Plain and Tall by Dakota Cockaday writing as Cassi O. Peia

Much Ado About Rutting by Sabrina Cross

The Spy Who Stung Me by Latrexa Nova

About the Author

Sabrina Cross (she/her) is a neurospicy 80's baby from the middle of nowhere Michigan, where she still lives with her cat. She came into her monster romance era early when she fell in love with Beast from the 1997's X-Men animated series. After discovering sentient object romance in early 2023, Sabrina decided to embrace what she calls her 'Hold My Beer' style of writing and gave into the lifelong dream of being an author. When not writing weird monster/sentient object smut, Sabrina can be found hanging out on social media (@authorsabrinacross), reading, or hoarding office supplies.

Also by Sabrina Cross

Yarn & Monsters Series

A True Love Spell Gone Wrong...

When four friends perform a true love spell, things go terribly wrong. Now they're locked into a deal with the devil and have only a year to find love and happiness or their souls are destined to face the flames. Armed with a demon guardian; Clover, Jasmine, Fern, and Violet are determined to beat the devil and save themselves. Except, this curse might be the best thing that's ever happened to them.

Corny: A F/F Candy Corn Romance

Snuggle: A M/F Demon Teddy Bear Romance

Tangled: A M/F Friends-To-Lovers Sentient Object Romance

Knotted: A M/F Demon Werewolf Romance

The Cursed Matchmaker Series

Never Piss off a witch. Or else you may find yourself trapped in a glory hole booth at an upscale sex club. But when the perfect couples hook up anonymously, Josh has no choice but to speak out and help them find love.

The Glory Whole Package

The Glory Whole Experiment

The Glory Whole Redemption

Retro Whimsy Series

Welcome to Retro Whimsy where nothing is as it seems and the owners know just what you need.

Getting Railed

Trogg Trouble

Game Girl

Ghostlight Falls - Shared World Series

Cooking Up A Demon

Planet WLN269 Needs Women - Shared World Series

Taken in by the Aliens

Much Ado About Rutting

Stand Alone Monster Romance

Christmas with the Monster

Can't Yeti Enough

Stand Alone Sentient Object Romance

Light Me Up

Pounded by the Pommel Horse

Sentient Pen15 from Outer Space

Knotty Broomsticks

www.ingramcontent.com/pod-product-compliance
Lightning Source LLC
Chambersburg PA
CBHW020046310726
48970CB00007B/2433